I0601817

I Know You Like
a Murder

Amy L. Sauder

The readers have spoken:

"This is SUCH a quirky meta mystery and I'm 100% on board." ~ Olivia J. Bennett, author of *A Cactus in the Valley*

"Absolutely amazing. My jaw literally dropped. So much hindsight." ~ Stephanie Gagnon

"Great. Now I wanna make a character that breaks the fourth wall and insults the audience. Thanks, Amy." ~ Megan Fatheree, author of *Dust to Dust* (plus more), cofounder of the #WritersSlumberIt tomfoolery

"Oh no. I love this murderer. So cheeky and clever. AH! Inner Turmoil." ~ Jennifer Esther Wieland, interior illustrator for this book

"It really felt like I was being pulled into the investigation." ~ Linda Heller

"Couched within innocent normal-sounding narrative, it becomes that much more jarring and creepy." ~ Jaclyn Lewis, curator and creative

"I don't get tripped up in whodunnits very often because I have read so many, so it was refreshing to be wrong this time." ~ Heather Reid

Cover design: AMBER&GRAPHICS
Interior illustrations: Jennifer Esther Wieland
Author photo: Yasmeen Hudson
Scripture reference: Young's Literal Translation

Copyright © 2018 Amy L. Sauder
All rights reserved.
ISBN 978-1-7323530-0-8
Library of Congress Control Number: 2018906681

for the readers and dreamers

Table of Contents

Cast of Characters

Madame Director. Strict with her theater. Indulgent with her pet projects.

Homeless Hag. One of Madame Director's pet projects. The ol' loon lowers the hood so you can't see a face, then sits in the back and snores.

Facilities Hawk. a.k.a. Facilities Manager. Paranoid as anything. Attends each rehearsal to ensure there's no damage to property, no ruckus, no snooping.

Shy Boy. Ex-boyfriend of the scriptwriter. He dumped her, and now her play is his lonesome chance at stardom. Poetic.

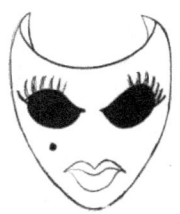

Makeup Artist. She's got attitude, but that's no surprise when a leading lady loses her spotlight.

Villains 1 & 2. Not necessarily the villains of this story, but villains within the script. Dark wings. Darker capes. Mythical creatures.

Cami's BFF. A yes-woman. Stage Manager, which only means she caters to Cami's every wish.

The one you've been waiting for: **Camille.** Or Cami now. The name change is for product branding or whatever. Washed up writer. Now scriptwriter and on top of that, leading lady. Madame Director allowed her to steal the spotlight, even though Cami has never performed on stage.

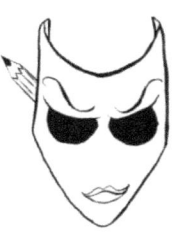

The 5 W's of Murder:

A narrator always gets to know the reader before spilling their deepest secret.

I am a murderer.

She was just a silly nothing of a girl until I made her rise to fame. A pennything. Was her name Chloe, Jess, Reanna? Doesn't matter, they all blend into one girl: my victim.

I imagine a dreary donut-glaze day at the station before I dropped murder in their laps. I'd like to say the coppers pounded down my door in their cliché little way, but really it was a nice rap-tap-tap. Like the children's ditty: *Skunk in the barnyard, pee-yew. Murder in the theater...for you...*

Clueless buffoons, more accustomed to traffic control than detective work. I wasn't considered suspect; as far as they knew, I was victim.

"Tell us what happened." "Did you notice anything out of the ordinary?" "Any odd or unusual behavior?" and the kicker: "Is there anyone who would have motive?"

"Don't we all," I said. "Don't we all hold a reason to kill."

I wasn't much help. Why would I be? I divulged a dozen motives to bait their sniffers a million directions, all but mine.

I don't think they liked me all that much. Whatever. I wasn't looking to impress. I was looking to distract. Once their curiosities turned elsewhere, I could move on to tell you, my now-avid readers, the story.

My story.

Our story.

If a tree falls and no one hears, does it make a sound? If a person is murdered and the tale is not told, did it happen?

And so, I have found my audience. Yes, you. Won't you read my story, sleuth it out? I take the role of murderer, now you fancy yourself a detective.

Sit down, cozy up. I'd offer you a cup of tea, but you may worry it's been poisoned, and you may be correct. But hold it, dear reader, don't twist your shirt in a bundle before I give you all the pieces.

What: death, cold and sudden

Where: the most dramatic place for murder, the theater

When: the top of Act III, naturally

Who: Too many names, there are too many names in the world. I only remember the one girl. Don't be indignant when you struggle to recall names, too.

No matter. I will choose some form of name to distinguish the lot. Let's call them:

Madame Director,

Homeless Hag,

Facilities Hawk,

Villains 1 & 2,

Shy Boy,

Makeup Artist,

and *Cami's BFF.*

But the one you're waiting for: *Camille.* Or Cami now, to be more relatable, likeable. Hear the sounds roll off your tongue: the name Cami skips playfully from your mouth, while the nasal sound of Camille bodes aloof, unapproachable. The name change is product branding or whatever.

She's a washed up writer. Now scriptwriter and also, get this, leading lady. Scooped that right up, and Madame Director allowed it, though Cami has never performed on stage.

Why: Cami got one of the useless English degrees and expected it was worth something. Interned at a publishing company, but they wouldn't look at her manuscript without an agent; and she couldn't interest an agent though she had an in with a publisher.

She'd tell that sob story, then with a twinkle in her eye promise that this theatrical production would put us all on the map.

Hopeful.

Deluded.

But I would make her keep that promise.

Alibis are useless here, because all of us, of course, were at the theater when it happened. As for motive, don't we all have something worth killing for?

If you were a Criminal Psychologist maybe you'd have this case wrapped up by now. Tell me, which character am I, the murderer?

But statistically speaking, you likely aren't a Criminal Psychologist, so here you are. Still reading, so many questions. You could hand this off to a Criminal Psychologist to solve. But I don't think you will. Not now. *It's not real*, you say. *It's a book.* You'll pore through this story looking for answers, intrigued by the tale, fascinated by death.

Okay, detectivize. Draw up a grid, write up characters and clues, cross off cleared suspects. Or whatever you crime buffs do. Maybe you have the cliché marker board to track your clues, or maybe you have the string linking ideas throughout a crime-solving room. You sure get off on this stuff, don't you?

So let's get to it. What I haven't told you yet is *How*. But I can't just tell you how she died. That's too easy. Too quick. Buckle up: you're in for a villainous monologue.

How It All Began:

Was it happenstance, fate, or some calculated plan that Madame Director and Cami both visited the library at precisely 2:38 in the afternoon on this particular Wednesday? In a small town with little to do, bumping into an old acquaintance is not uncommon.

"Camille Winters," Madame Director barked, much louder than one ever should in a library.

"Ah! Fancy seeing you here. Oh, but I'm not Camille anymore. Cami. Cami Sommers is my pen name, once I publish. You like?"

Cami has a bubbly personality – yet it was overcompensated, still coaxing the friendly banter from her cutthroat Camille shell.

Madame Director had taught Cami, back when she was Camille. Camille had been terse, prone to turn her nose at any hint of small talk, but the new improved Cami was all perky jabber-jabber.

Cami gushed about the injustice of her publishing misfortunes, and Madame Director found her next pet project.

"Write my theatrical production. Experience under your belt. We'll show everyone that literature and theater are a perfect pairing."

Cami forced a giggle. "You're still harping on that? Silly schoolgirl days."

Madame Director had lost her shot at tenure when the Theater & Writing Dialogue class was cut. Cami witnessed the career setback – one of the last students of the course – so she caught the bitter jab.

Still, Cami's optimism won out, giddy as can be at another shot to live off her writing. An exchange of phone numbers. A suggestion of coffee. They left the library in separate directions – Cami with a bounce in her step, Madame Director with a smirk on her face.

How You Think You're Picking Up on Something But You're Actually Not:

"It's wrong, all wrong."

Cami already had her story, so now she only needed a script. She furiously typed the edits and found thousands of errors. "No! Only perfect will convince everyone."

The meticulous ferocity continued through the coffee meeting, casting, rehearsals... Even opening night she would be changing words or gestures.

"It's not right yet!" But of course it wasn't right – it didn't contain murder.

So when she wouldn't get a clue and write it in, I improvised.

You may be wondering how I know all these sordid details. I can't possibly be everywhere at once. And you're right.

I come up with my own version of the tale. That's what cops always hear from a witness anyhow: an individual's personal version. You have mine, take it or leave it.

Some of the details I was present for; some are overheard. An entrusted whisper morphs into a public declaration through the great powers of poor acoustics. There are no secrets in this building. Until a murder happened, everyone assumed they knew everyone else like their own self. You don't have to read minds to consider yourself a worthy psychic in the theater.

And then of course there's the parts of the story I make up, put my own spin on. Some inferring and conjecture, some dramatic interpretation. Creative license.

Did you miss the "I'm a murderer" part?

Of course my tale can't be trusted. I'm psychotic. Maybe delusional.

Certainly unreliable.

How the Script Plays Out:

Now that we're on the same page, let me tell you about the script. *What Walks Among Us* was to be the next big thing. Cami assured us we would make millions and sell out every show. Hyperbole, I suppose.

The story introduces a fantastical girl with majestic wings. Let's call her Penny, because as I said, she was a pennything before I brought her fame.

Misunderstood by ordinary humans, Penny befriends demonic winged creatures – none other than Villains 1 & 2.

When the demons discover Penny's powers, they believe she is the one prophesied to destroy their regime. Penny is once again ostracized – this time not by mere mortals, but by a dark version of her own kind.

As any fairy tale would have it, the setback only triggers Penny's heroism. Hiding her wings beneath a cloak, she disguises herself as a "Normal" and rallies the humans to take down the demonic ones.

Shy Boy is captain of Penny's human army. He is quite taken with Penny, but of course does not know her winged secret.

At the climax of the story, the demonic birds tear through Penny's human army, and all hope is lost.

But wait. Penny climbs a tower above the ruckus and removes her cloak. The umber wings spread to a 12 foot wingspan. Winged Penny is glowing atop the tower – that's right, like some archangel in all its glory.

The humans cover their faces, blinded. The stage fades to black, then reverts to a soft glow. Of the demonic creatures, only tarred feathers and a great stench remain.

Talk about a messiah complex, am I right?

Cami had a charming way of turning things to her advantage, even a simple community play. The bird creatures were supposed to be what walks among us, but what really walks among us is a lunatic narcissist.

You may notice there that opportunity for murder abounds in Act III. Chaos of battle and brightness and blackout and – oh, it's beautiful. Simply perfection.

Careful, Penny. Hopes and dreams will be the death of you. I'll murder you, *Penny, for your thoughts.*

How the Cast of Characters Came to Be:

All the usual people auditioned. But this time, it was the *un*usual people cast.

As you can expect, the routine female lead (from henceforth and evermore known as Makeup Artist) did not land the lead role. Or any acting role. She treated the stage like a runway, with a confident stride and stretched neck. The audition was flawless.

Madame Director smiled wider than her own face, terribly proud of the peacock performance. "Thank you, Terri. That was excellent." Let's pretend Terri is her name. Or maybe it was Carla, can't be sure.

"No need for everyone to wait and wonder," Cami whispered, though all could hear because acoustics. "We should assign the roles as we go."

Madame Director nodded, a ruse of obliging her pet. "Yes, but we should consult with each other first."

"I have a vision for this production, a vision that can't be compromised. I value your feedback" – Cami said it sweet as syrup and honey fountains – "but I firmly believe that this actress cannot convey the fantastical atmosphere when her personality is so down-to-earth."

Then Cami, in a voice for all to hear: "We can assign her to hair and makeup. Her contouring is exquisite."

Madame Director cocked her head. "Alright, Cami, I'll follow your lead. Let's see your literary vision on stage."

Pet project that she is, Cami would see the intermingling of literature and theater if Madame Director had any say.

In Cami's college days, a scandal led to silly gossip that writers and drama geeks don't mix. The introverts and the extroverts. The quirky and the outlandish. This controversy meant that only a few students registered for the joint Dialogue elective, and ever since then a barrier existed between the English and Theater cliques.

So now Madame Director gave Cami reins to decisions generally relegated to Director. Besides, certain directorial choices make for minimal impact in a community play since budget and casting are meager.

And that's the story of how the female lead became Makeup Artist instead.

In addition to one miffed Makeup Artist, Cami made other surprising choices. A couple of reliable bumbling redheads were denied any role in the production. With little leading talent, presumably their only role could be in the cast of humans, yet their hair would detract from the pure majesty of the bird creatures. So Cami said.

That still didn't explain why they weren't chosen for stage design or lighting, but I have my own idea. Cami believed redheads would detract from the true star of the show: herself. Her drab and doldrum locks were no match for the shimmering copper. Shallow, superficial girl.

While many auditions were quite hurriedly dismissed, others were a surprising choice. Shy Boy had barely begun his monotone ramblings before Cami interrupted. "Thank you, *ex-boyfriend*, for your time. I don't need to see anymore."

He was not only humiliated, but positive he'd see no role in the production.

I suppose you want the backstory now. Can't simply keep your paws out of someone else's love life, can you? Must know all the dirty details...

Fine. Don't need to tell me twice.

When Cami centered her campaign for Student Body President on the infamous theater/literature debacle, Shy Boy Theater major took it a little personal and ended their relationship in his bumbling way.

"I, uhh, I don't know what's, what's going on. I'm Theater and you're, uhh, English, and this campaign thing, how does that work for us? How? I don't see it, I mean, I don't know how, uhh..."

Cami – Camille then, but with either name never short on words – was abrupt. "You're right. My campaign, this separation between the classes, our relationship. It doesn't mix. It's okay. I'll get over it." She brushed past him and raced through the halls, so he couldn't see just how much the breakup affected her.

She was elusive back then, but all drama queen up-in-your-face now.

Of course Cami would end his theater dreams like he ended her romantic dreams, everyone figured. But Cami surprised us all: "You're hired. I mean, no pay of course, but sure. You'll be Captain of the Human Army."

Shy Boy drooped his head and sulked off stage, as if he'd lost his dignity rather than landed the most prestigious male role in an obscure community production. Pitiful lad.

Villains 1 & 2 were selected without a thought. They brought their own elaborate costuming and genuine slice-and-dice swords for practice. Cast and crew would huddle around and watch, the worst and best of us hoping for an incidental injury.

Facilities Hawk and Madame Director frowned at the danger, but acquiesced. It seemed relatively harmless when signed waivers would prevent a lawsuit. If they had known murder was in the making, they may have banned the weapons.

Of course, perhaps I the murderer am in fact Madame Director or Facilities Hawk. If so, then I merely allowed the weapons as a diversion, using the "it seemed harmless at the time" reasoning to throw you off track.

Don't get too cozy in your postulations.

Not once did Villains 1 & 2 remove their makeup on set or backstage, as if they embodied the creatures in the script. The black and silver streaks and the outlandish swooping hairstyles were part of them as much as their elusive stance. They remained aloof from the rest of the cast throughout the production – mythological creatures that we mere mortals couldn't begin to fathom.

Cami admired their passion, imagining it nearly akin to her own. She even gave a standing ovation for the audition.

Oh yes, back to auditions. Imagine the moment when two kindred spirits meet, the sun and moon at the brink of eclipse, simply kissing before snuffing each other out. That's what you're about to witness.

Cami's BFF never met Cami until auditions, yet came to worship her much too quickly. The girl had auditioned at every community play, yet her mousy hair and timid voice were best served in the wings.

Cami took to her, though.

"Madame Director tells me you are a committed thespian," Cami said. "Not once late, tipsy, or contrary. That's exactly the type of person to take on the responsibility of

Stage Manager. I need someone I can rely on to make my vision reality."

Of course Cami would cozy up to a little shadow person, someone who would bob her head and trail Cami's feet and turn no eyes. She would ever be at Cami's hip, yet vanish from sight in the glow of Cami's charisma. And Cami preferred it that way.

Cami's BFF gave a submissive curtsy and smile, then tottered off the stage, entranced by the managerial position she could never have earned.

The promotion meant little, though. The role mainly constituted of mixing together "Cami's Concoction", the name we gave to her pretentious blend of warm water, pineapple juice, and Manuka honey.

"Make certain it's my Manuka honey, not that cheap convenience store crap," Cami would say. "My voice requires star treatment."

But Cami's persnickety demands were no biggie for her BFF, who was eager to please.

She was quick to help in Cami's schemes, though I must confess that Cami's schemes proved rather tame: gathering the cast to dream of fame together, last-minute changes to the script and costumes, teasing words here and there only to see Shy Boy blush.

Cami acted the epitome of perfection, and for the most part, adoration followed her like a deluded puppy.

Cami inspired everyone who met her. She made people believe they had a role, not only in the play, but in the world. She had us all convinced that this meager town play, which only one small paper may cover, would somehow lead us to fame and Broadway.

We were elated. In Cami's eyes, we could all be, *would* all be, legends.

She made me believe it. This production could change the world, or our world at least. But Cami's writing couldn't accomplish that, and certainly not the cast's acting abilities. This I knew. So I found my own way to make her hopes reality.

But I couldn't take any chances. Haven't you noticed I'm far too clever to pull the hypothetical trigger myself? You must know I had an accomplice, that I am merely the puppet master pulling the strings of an all-too-eager follower.

Adjust your suspect list accordingly – this murder is more complex than you're even now ready to accept. Trust me. But also don't, because why trust someone this disturbed, what are you thinking?

How Murder Isn't So Bad:

Of course I'm selfish. But I didn't only think of myself with this murder.

This may come as a surprise, but I'm a vigilante, a public servant. Misunderstood, yes. Considered heartless though I have the greater good in mind.

Like a judge sentencing the lethal injection of a menace, or a mayor taxing the masses to repave pothole-ridden roads. "No prophet is accepted in his own country" (Luke 4.24). If the Messiah himself was doubted, how could I expect to be spared?

We as cast and crew are community, but I can tell you our individual interests. I can tell you that murder benefits more than destroys.

Shy Boy wants a quiet purpose. Villains 1 & 2 want attention – think Lady Gaga. Cami's BFF wants affirmation, and Madame Director wants to make the world better through art. Homeless Hag wants shelter and security. Facilities Hawk wants stability. And all Cami wants is recognition.

Six birds, meet one deadly stone.

Why, even you dear reader would benefit from this murder. Without it, wouldn't this tale be a bore? Would you not throw this book across the room if we came to the end and I said, "Haha, kidding, they all lived long and healthy lives"? Would you not give up if you knew the story led to no demise?

You benefit from murder as much as the rest of us. You are, dare I say, entertained by murder. Now who's the psychopath?

Wait. No.

Let me qualify that statement for you... You are positively titillated by *fictitious* murder.

Better?

Are you justified in your pleasure now? Are you back atop your high horse, separate from the likes of sadist me?

The point is, I can give us all what we want: cast, crew, even you and especially Cami.

And of course me. I can't wait for Cami to get gone. I am egotistical, so there has to be something in it for me.

Oh, wait, let's not forget the one person who will not find their heart's desire: Facilities Hawk. Life is about to become quite unstable for him. The murder and the blood and the crime tape that blocks all entry. The vulturous reporters that cannot be satiated. The rumors of a haunted facility. The teenage break-ins and vandalism. The "For Sale" sign that withers through the years.

No, this isn't Hawk's cup of tea. He could create a lucrative attraction, recruiting actors for an avant-garde haunted house or a mystery dinner. But he isn't the progressive type, into fads or trends or even theatricality (the irony here is striking).

Still, overall, I hope you can agree that my choice is for the good of the community I'm entrenched in. Now can I get on with this murder without a fuss already? After all, one individual's loss can't be considered over the gain of all others, can it?

How Rehearsals Got Out of Hand:

With Madame Director attempting to guide green Cami on her first show, rehearsals were anything but ordinary. You probably picked up on that. The cast and crew picked up on it during auditions and still weren't prepared for the rookie treatment.

The cast found it impossible to record the myriad script changes. The human army would take the stage too late, or Shy Boy would proclaim (mutter) his affections before the third Act's denouement.

Each script contained varying scribbles and margin notes written by cast, crew, or most commonly by the great high Cami herself. Yet no one took the time to replicate scribbles across scripts, and the group communicated little, so each cast member inevitably had their own unique draft.

Only Cami ever claimed to keep track of what happens when, but she had to make it up as she went.

Through all the confusion, we admired Cami's resolve, how she fought for our chance. She was our best shot at a hit show. Her nerves were simply frayed with the pressure of her dream. Our dream.

Huddle discussions of our names in lights were the norm before practice, after practice, between scenes, and at lunch.

Cami was an incessant ray of sunshine at any dreamerly rendezvous. "Just wait 'til Brenda the Good Witch of the West grabs ahold of you munchkins." Laughable, but quaint. She tried to be a relevant actress, but Broadway obviously wasn't her forte.

Really the only time Cami wasn't endearing was during rehearsal. Everything must be perfect, and nothing ever was.

Cami demanded the best from herself, though only she might call it any good, and she demanded the best of us as well. We can't fault her for that. We can't fault her for changing an imperfect script, even if the timing was not ideal.

Villains 1 & 2 didn't care about script changes. They marched to their own drum. Their scripts were clean as can be, because they simply made all their acting improv.

Cami gave a polite smile with sharp eyes every time they went off script, or basically the entire show. Still, their improvisations proved to be the best part, of higher caliber than any of Cami's scribbles.

Villains 1 & 2 were the only ones confident in acting out their characters when opening night arrived. Everyone else scrambled and stumbled and hoped they were using the final version of stage entrances and dialogue.

Even Cami wasn't at her A game. As if she knew that her moment was imminent, that her long-winded dream speeches were twisted into a death scene for the grand debut. Whether the performance is remarkable or catastrophic – we're making headlines for an altogether different reason.

How the Red Herring Flies:

Yeah yeah, it's not a bird, it's a fish. But everything hits the fan when fish fly. Just ask the Homeless Hag.

Homeless people aren't only the obnoxious snore in the background. They actually have a backstory and motive and character arc.

If you're an avid reader or a tiny bit of a film buff, you'll say the Homeless Hag is a red herring. And not only because this scene title says "red herring". You know that the most suspicious character is innocent in all fiction, and who is more suspicious than a Homeless Hag with no business in a theater?

Plus in any good story, the murderer isn't portrayed as some cliché hobo. The social justice movement would have a heyday. "Of course, all the high-falutin' working class citizens are off the hook while the homeless charity case freeloader is the thug accused of murder," they'd say. Can't happen, else the book would burn.

For that reason, Homeless Hag is assigned the role of obvious red herring. But there's more to Homeless Hag than meets the eye. Turn the hypothetical camera lens off center stage, zoom in on the audience of one, and peek through the mangy hood.

In some alternate universe, this rag-a-buffoon may have been described as a lady. There was once a time that she kept each hair in place and had a semi-successful career as the administrative assistant for the college's English department.

Back then everyone knew her face, but few took the time to learn her name. One personal tragedy after another led to a rarely laundered hoodie and the back row of a rundown theater, losing touch with all her colleagues save one: Madame Director.

Homeless Hag chose this particular location for more than shelter. Truth be told (*Do you believe me more when I say it's truth?*), the Hag stuck around to see Cami flop. Nothing cheers a lowlife like seeing the height from which enemies fall.

Okay, that may be a little overstated, for Homeless Hag and Cami weren't enemies. But come on, did Cami really think her campus presidential platform would garner friends, after she divided people like cards and stacked the deck in her favor?

Cami's internship attempts were riding on an aggressive résumé, application, essay... She was Camille back then, remember, and Camille was bullheaded, tenacious, more content with collateral damage than the rebranded, personal-transformation, "all in this together" sing-song Cami.

If Camille needed a killer paper for the internship, is it any surprise that she would document the school scandal when damning evidence comes to light?

A slew of emails and a few saucy texts surfaced, proving assistant-turned-hobo had fooled around with none other than Star Student of the theater.

Questions erupted like a volcano. You know how it works – the entire school speculated the most fanciful stories. Did he earn his straight A's from book prowess or anatomical prowess? Were his recurring lead roles due to the power of seduction? How far up the chain did the corruption go? How many "powers that be" fell under his sway?

Star Student's girlfriend was distraught by the side-chick competition. Star Student no longer walked among friends, but with head hanging to hide his cherub face. And the condemned admin assistant, with time, transformed into the laid-off homeless grump that haunted the theater with snores.

Cami was elected Student Body President on the wings of the scandal, since her Star Student competition lost his chance.

But her blatant disregard didn't end there. Cami documented it all. She wrote a paper expounding on the Theater/English split, the scandal, and the broader themes of authority and seduction. And of course that paper would land her the internship at her dream publishing company.

Cami saw the opportunity in the calamity, and that made some enemies. It was no shock that the administrative Hag was laid off at the end of the scandalous semester. It was even less shocking that Star Student didn't return the following year.

I'm not saying the Homeless Hag is here to take out Cami. I'm just saying she probably won't be upset when it happens. Homeless Hag's fall caused Cami's rise, and maybe for once she'd appreciate a role reversal.

How to Get a Gun to a Stage Fight:

Easy: have a psycho ex.

Cami saw a chance to cozy up to Shy Boy. It wasn't some sort of back and forth flirting that lasted weeks; she simply skipped up to him one day, wrapped her arms around the poor lad, and planted a kiss. Subtlety is not her strongsuit.

Shy Boy gave an impeccable response. Take note, for when a fine specimen seduces you:

"I got a gun," he said. Overkill, ya think?

Cami cackled. "Aren't you the charmer."

The cast and crew were riveted by the live soap opera.

"I did," Shy Boy said. "It-it got out of hand before, and I n-needed to protect myself. You're so...so..."

"Passionate? Ambitious? Dare I say, alluring?" Cami squeezed closer and made her voice husky. "I know what I want, and I go for it. We're all going for it, so keep your head in the game, ya hear? Forget the gun."

Shy Boy blushed. He took her hand and moved it lower.

"Oh, so scandalous," Cami said, but it wasn't scandal. It was a calculated weapon. It was cold passion. Passion that froze the heart of any in its grip. The gun.

"You brought it with you?" She grabbed it by the barrel, and he sucked in his breath. Cami yanked the gun from his pants.

"It's not loaded," he assured the crowd. "I ju-just needed to feel s-safe."

"Good job." Cami raised her eyebrows. "You labeled yourself a lunatic reject that's gonna shoot up the theater."

Shy Boy pointed his toe, infatuated with the floor instead of Cami. "I ju-"

"Load it." Cami's command was a surprise.

The audience of cast and crew gasped right on cue. Way to defuse the situation.

Madame Director decided now was apt timing to get involved. "Cami, I think we can put that away now."

"Load it," Cami insisted, extending the gun to Shy Boy. "Prove you're not going to shoot this place up."

Shy Boy shoved his hands in his pockets. Fiddling. They were there. We all knew.

"It's okay," Cami said. "You're not going to shoot us. Load the gun and prove it."

Shy Boy pulled his hand out of his pocket, clasped. He opened his palm, a nest of death. Three cold bullets.

"I only have three," he said, "I swear, I wouldn't. I wouldn't..."

"So just three of us are dead," Cami said. "Comforting. Let me see." She used the sleeve of her dress and picked up a bullet.

Cami perked her head and batted her lashes. "Is this one for me? Aww, you shouldn't have..."

In an instant she was back to coaxing. "Load the gun," and he did. He did just that.

"Don't!" Madame Director stepped in again.

"Stay back. I got this." Cami said. Then to Shy Boy: "Shoot. Prove you won't hit us. Waste the bullets on the tower."

Everyone was scurrying in a jiffy.

Madame Director stepped forward to stop the idea from materializing, but too late.

Shy Boy closed his eyes and aimed. I say aimed, but with eyes closed it was arbitrary. Pop, pop, and off went the bullets. One to the floor, and one oh-so-lucky shot to the tower.

Facilities Hawk was none too pleased.

Cami scooped up the remaining evidence before anyone recovered.

"Please, I'm not..." Shy Boy's eyes glistened.

Cami hushed him. "We all know you're not crazy now."

Makeup Artist whipped out her phone to call the cops, but Cami stopped her. "Don't. He'll go to jail. They'll think he's a killer on the verge."

And we all – well, we all decided not to speak of it again. Shy Boy wouldn't really hurt anyone, would he? Surely not.

The groupthink settled over the theater. We do not speak of this day. We protect our own. We keep Shy Boy from going over the edge.

How Motives Fell Like Dominos:

Besides backstory, who has motive for murder in this sweet group of dreamers? Even a less than astute reader can see it's not all fun and hopeful starry eyes in the drama club. Backstabbers, gossips, divas, hustlers, and social climbers will smash you like a stinkbug without a second glance.

I almost believed Shy Boy and Cami would hook up again with all their teasing. Shy Boy would blush and even crack a smile on occasion. Cami would have arranged a tryst, but he was slow to warm up.

Cami was a natural flirt though, and would latch on to any prey in her general vicinity.

One rehearsal she approached Villains 1 & 2 for a chat. They startled like squirrels on the highway, but recovered quickly.

"Hey," Cami said, "could you show the lady in makeup how to make my red eyeshadow match your silver cat-eye look? That would go over better for, ya know, the complementary contrast of our mythological creatures, if you could teach her."

Villains 1 & 2 gave tight smiles and a nod. Cami bounced with glee, as if she'd been nominated prom queen, and gave each Villain a peck on the cheek.

"Hooray! I knew you'd rescue me from this catastrophe." Cami framed her face with her hands. "Lifesavers. Thank you."

No biggie, you'd think, but the dominoes were lined up, and Cami had knocked over the first. Had she realized Shy Boy would see the exchange?

Shy Boy glowered at Villain 1. "Manslut," Shy Boy mumbled. Only, of course, acoustics, so everyone heard.

Cami gave Shy Boy an exaggerated pout face. "Be nice."

Shy Boy's face warmed at the scrutiny. "He just, agh, he always gets...gets the limelight... Always."

Think it through: a thespian wearing a makeup mask 24/7, opposite a slouching wallflower. Might I just say *of course* Villain 1 gets more limelight than Shy Boy.

Not sure why this was up for debate, but Shy Boy had more to say for once. In fact, he had the perfect plot twist for our little story.

"I can't...I can't catch a break," Shy Boy said. "You bounce him outta school, and he still gets the ladies all the while."

Talk about a blast from the past. Cami covered her mouth, but couldn't resist a giggle escaping. Poor Shy Boy scurried at the mockery, not to return 'til the following day.

"No way," Cami said. "Are you two seriously undercover crashing my show?"

Cami was positively giddy. She waltzed between the Villains; their makeup did little to protect their identity now. "That desperate for an act, ya cover up your pretty face and make your ex watch?" Cami jabbed a finger out at the audience, or should I say Homeless Hag, but only a loud snore responded.

Villains 1 & 2 scowled, but Shy Boy was right. Cozied up to their own whistleblower on stage were Star Student and his girl. Gotta hand it to them, disguised all this time, the commitment.

All the world's a stage, after all.

Cami seemed to agree, clapping her hands. "Delightful. Positively delightful, two secret agents. You two, I hope you know, bygones and all that. I've put the past behind, and we're moving to brighter days together."

Cami patted Villain 2's cheek. Villain 2 scrunched her nose, but Cami acted oblivious.

Despite the figurative unmasking, Villains 1 & 2 neglected to remove their literal masks. In fact, they pretended as if they'd never been found out. Still silent as mimes outside their character lines, still refusing to remove the makeup, still inseparable.

Speaking of makeup, they didn't forget Cami's request. Villains 1 & 2 approached Makeup Artist to discuss Cami's eyeshadow.

"No! No, no, no!" Makeup Artist slammed her brushes on the vanity. The former leading lady – who need I remind you was assigned backstage due to some crap claim of exceptional contouring – was not interested in a makeup tutorial now. "She wants to insult my work, she can say it to my face."

Makeup Artist barged onstage mid-scene, but all stopped when alerted to the ruckus.

"Cami!" Makeup Artist pushed Cami to stage left and gripped Cami's chin. So close to the throat. "My makeup is exquisite. Your face is the problem, hear me?"

Cami gritted her teeth under Makeup Artist's grip. "Think carefully. Everyone is watching." She blinked. Perhaps tears finally threatened her rose-colored world.

But an audience doesn't deter someone who basks in the limelight.

Makeup Artist smirked. "Eyeshadow won't make your show a lick better. You want red streaks? I can arrange that. I would *love* to see you red all over, but the only thing that would make this show newsworthy is if it was me on the tower with outstretched wings while you lie below begging for one. last. breath." She said the last three words like separate sentences, the drama queen.

Makeup Artist said her piece and released her grip. She was the second person to storm out in the final days of Cami's rule.

How Cami Got a Frenemy:

Eventually Cami's BFF raised a smug nose at her own puppetry. Who knew sucking up to the tippy top would go to her head? She took the role of Stage Manager as if Director of the Royal Shakespeare Company itself. Buddying up with Cami, they were two peas and iron against iron, a deadly razor pea soup debacle.

I digress.

It started sweet and innocent. Cami's BFF tailed her from dawn to dusk. They entered the theater giggling and left the theater whispering. (*"Finally! A moment alone with our Siamese-twin thoughts."*)

But one Siamese grew too big for the other's britches, demanding nourishment the other craved. Scriptwriter and leading lady wasn't enough; Cami must run the show backstage, too. Madame Director had long ago succumbed to her pet project's reign. Cami had one more queen yet to dethrone.

The night before dress rehearsal, Cami decreed that the set was the wrong color. "Not golden yellow. Honey yellow complements the costume hues."

Which meant a late night repainting for the crew, none too happy. Cami softened the blow by volunteering to help, but the good vibes didn't last.

Facilities Hawk hovered, extra grouchy from the long hours. He busied himself repairing the tower's marginally loose board caused by the gunshot.

Klutzy Cami shouldn't have even been there, absent-minded enough to open the paint can in the closet and carry it brimming full to the set.

"Don't!" Facilities Hawk's outburst made her start, and it was too late. The bucket plastered her dress and pooled on the floor.

Hawk was now a complete curmudgeon, abandoning his toolbox to instead scrub floors like Cinderella. Meanwhile, the vain stepsister Cami shut herself in the bathroom, dousing her outfit with paint cleaner in hopes of salvaging it.

Cami only joined the cleaning party again in order to apologize for her early exit: "I am terribly sorry for this disastrous event, and right on the heels of our breakout debut, too. But I must hurry and put my dress in the wash. It's my favorite, ya see?"

Cami's BFF volunteered to stay late with Facilities Hawk to clean – a sweet gesture, but how long does it take to wipe a puddle compared to repainting the set honey instead of golden?

Of course there was a hissy fit next morn. Night to day, best friends turned frenemies. Suddenly there wasn't enough space for Cami and her BFF in the same city, let alone the same theater.

They arrived to dress rehearsal in a huff. Stars too bright to bear the sight of each other, I suppose. Someone was bound to get sick of Cami's dictatorship at some point.

Everyone completed the dress rehearsal on tiptoe and eggshells. Even Homeless Hag couldn't snore away the day – on the edge of her seat, ready to escape at a moment's notice, as if a greater chill had claimed the theater than the chill outdoors.

Madame Director had already deferred to her pet projects running the show. This day, Cami's BFF directed while Cami sulked.

There were plenty of catty women eager for their moment to butcher the leading role on Cami's behalf. The show must go on.

Meanwhile, Cami strolled the audience aisles, praying through each row to the gods of glory that we all may be saved. She wore the winged cloak, as if hiding a secret of her own from those who prefer the mundane to the extraordinary.

Sulking didn't require her voice to project, so Cami traded her usual Manuka concoction for water bottles from the crew's mini-fridge. (Cami wasn't the only diva in the lot of thespians. Room temperature water was demanded by all the stage performers, to protect their voice. On the other hand, the backstage crew required condensation on their drinks.)

When Cami walked the row above Homeless Hag, she whiffed the air, crinkled her nose.

The animosity was thick, like the crumpled hood of that snorefest stinkbomb. Homeless Hag glared – at Cami, not at what I just called her in my narration. Homeless Hag isn't reading the story, silly, you are.

"What's the smell?" Homeless Hag shocked us with her booming voice before mumbling, "...what the cat dragged in."

"You're one to talk," Cami said. "Smelling your own self more'n likely."

Homeless Hag pushed to her feet and stared Cami down. "I never..." She shook her head and hobbled out.

Cami shrugged and continued meandering, refusing to act or direct. Really the show was better without the dictatorial control freak, even absent a proper leading lady.

Dress rehearsal went swimmingly, besides the lack of murder, of course. That oversight would be corrected the following day.

How Murder I Wrote:

Picture it: the jitters of opening night coupled with the animosity of the painting fiasco.

Cami's BFF refused to help after dropping the wings into Cami's unsuspecting hands. No worries though. Cami naturally reverted to barking orders at everyone else in her general vicinity. Like the world is her slave. Pah!

Shy Boy scurried to fetch hairpins while Villain 2 blotted the blush that Makeup Artist had smeared in vengeance across Cami's face. Meanwhile, Makeup Artist was assigned to keeping Manuka water at the ready.

A number of the crew members had taken ill, so Madame Director pulled double duty, handling the props and set pieces.

Utter chaos.

But no worries. Today I murder. I murder for you, darling readers.

You've wanted this. From the beginning, you've been waiting to see how it all goes down, down, down...

And this is our moment.

Acts I and II were pitiful, but aren't they always mere build-up to the finale?

The audience would sneak glances at their phones. It was to be expected; though the story was quite enchanting, the acting was subpar and the script mediocre.

But I would grab their attention yet. Those phones would whip out, not to scroll the latest news or text the latest beau, but to bear witness to blood and mayhem.

Finally, the crowning moment. The moment you waited an entire book for. Have you been watching closely?

The war against the humans waged strong. Hope was lost – for the pithy acting, as well as the battle. Yet an angelic act would save the day as the tides of battle turn.

Call the shots, reader. Detectivize. Who is the villainous head honcho mastermind, and who is the eager, willing accomplice?

In the trenches of battle, Cami neared her moment atop the tower. As the stage went black, she slipped backstage to replace the cloak with outspread wings.

"My Manuka water!" Her shout had to be loud enough for the audience to hear. She threw aside the cloak.

"Sshh," Madame Director reminded.

"Why," Cami whispered, still urgent. "Why is my Manuka water not here? Where is it?"

"Where should it be?"

"Right next to the stage. I put it here since positively no one is helping today." A dig at Cami's BFF, who ordinarily waited with bottle in hand for Cami's backstage appearances.

Madame Director scanned the area. "It must have been moved. No drinks where they can spill." She spied the bottle by the makeup and costumes.

"Ah!" Madame Director retrieved the drink while Cami adjusted her wings.

"Finally." Cami rolled her eyes. "The battle has been too long. It's time. Time to bring down the house."

She gulped the water like her defining moment depended on hydration. But it was too fast, the effects so strong.

Cami sputtered and spit the concoction, convulsing. Manuka water, bile, and what was later identified as paint cleaner spewed from her mouth.

Cami collapsed with just enough energy to brush hair from her face and struggle out of the wings.

It was all a blur then.

Let's see, how did it happen? Was it Heather, Sandy, Jen? Doesn't matter. Some stagehand or understudy was hurried into the wings, makeup slabbed on, a rush job. Some nobody was thrust up the tower, while Cami puked backstage.

A nameless face trotted up the steps – careful, dear – rushing right to where the bloodthirsty accomplice wanted her.

Perhaps she had a parent, a friend, a lover in the seats, cheering her on. Perhaps she had great Broadway dreams on the verge of coming true.

But all that would be ripped away, for the greater good, remember.

As our sacrificial substitute entered the spotlight, as the audience turned their yawning gaze back to the pinnacle, the actual murder began.

How did you do it?

How did you do it, reader?

Was it a slight nudge off the ledge, or is that too cliché for your tastes? Perhaps a simple wing malfunction to lose her footing. Did a gunshot paint the walls with gruesome spatter, or do you prefer a sword that pools the blood so neatly? Or perhaps poison, to keep the scene tidy. Did you set the stage alight in smoky inferno, to hear the drumbeat of evacuation? Or did you get personal with a wrench or tool to beat her down?

The poor penny lass thought rightly it was her moment of glory, but she didn't realize glory requires death. She didn't realize you waited atop the tower.

You knew it was coming. I groomed you. You wanted to see it.

However it happened, whatever you imagined – you killed her, reader.

You devoured the words, the ominous promises, the hope of the macabre. Turning page after page, you brought some obscure character closer to death.

For your own pleasure.

Because *it's only a story*, you said.

But I, Camille Winters, could not have done it without you, my darling reader.

I put on the role of Cami Sommers, sweet, darling, misunderstood victim. And you fell for it, didn't you?

You fell for it as I created a group with reasonable motives to kill. Jilted ex, jilted BFF, jilted performers, jilted faculty.

Even *you* would have been fine with Cami's death, and let's be real: I didn't like her either. I much prefer Camille.

Thanks to you, I can be rid of the sickly sweet Cami Sommers and put on the aloof Camille Winters again. Goodbye to doting inspirational Cami, and hello to conniving aspirational Camille.

The Camille who cozied up to some nobody theater major to access Star Student's phone. The Camille who forged emails and texts to fake a school scandal. The Camille who arranged for Shy Boy to dump her (thank goodness, it couldn't come soon enough!). The Camille who rose to the challenge of student president and publishing intern. Because of the sacrifices I am willing to force others to make on my behalf.

But I wasn't without sacrifices either. As Camille I had to be cozy with loser Shy Boy. Yech. As Cami I had to play nice with my BFF and the rest of the cast. Double yech.

Then I had to pull a bait-and-switch: create enemies out of colleagues. Allow the prissy Makeup Artist to strangle me without a fight. Spill paint on my pretend-favorite dress. I even had to poison myself. Murder doesn't come without a cost.

The understudy or whoever was gone, dead, nothing to be done for her now. But I had been the intended victim, poor thing.

After coughing up all the paint cleaner I allowed myself to ingest, I was doted on. The deceased was a blip on the newsworthy radar. All the cameras and interviews were directed toward the living target: me.

I would be questioned by police to identify suspects. Don't worry, I didn't rat you out. In fact, throughout the story we've created a perfect scapegoat.

If you sliced the victim to pieces, Villains 1 & 2 with their swords are a perfect diversion. If you burned Penny alive, no worries; I've spilled gasoline on seats in the general vicinity of Homeless Hag. I planted Facilities Hawk's tools by the tower, Shy Boy's bullets in the set, and the poisoned Manuka water near Makeup Artist's vanity.

I've made them all suspect. We all know my BFF was last handling my wings, and at her bitter resignation from the role of lapdog to boot. Plus, I even poured laxative into the crew's water bottles, so they'd be stuck home and Madame Director would be a little more up close and personal with stage work.

Why, I dare say, in whichever way you chose to murder our victim, you selected who would be arrested by the bumbling cops in our stead. How delightful.

Now I write a book, garner my fame and fortune. But an authoress is nothing without her reader.

I needed you. If a tree falls and no one hears, does it make a sound? If a murder is written but never read, did it happen?

But this *fictional* town, as you would call it, now has one less character. Each page you turned a death sentence.

And if you re-read it, there would be one less. And another. Perhaps next time it's Rachel, or Fiona, or Lacey. Eventually we run out of females and throw a guy up there with a wig. Want to slaughter a town until there's only you and me left?

Because every time a reader finishes this book, another character dies.

A narrator always gets to know the reader before spilling their deepest secret.

~Interview with a Reader~

Tell us what happened.

How did she die?

...

...

...

Are you sure?

...

...

...

Turn back to page 57. Please confirm.

...

...

...

~The cause of death~
~has not yet been released to the public~

~New from Amy L. Sauder~

Julia Trencher has died. Twice. But Geppetto's
Circus of Strange Marvels offers hope of others like
her—a place she could be welcomed, celebrated
even. She didn't know it would lead to herself and
the circus vanishing amidst a mysterious fire.

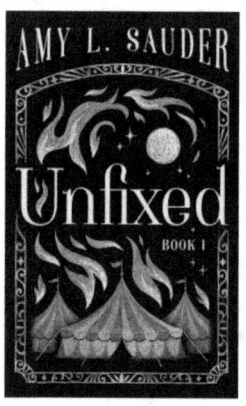

Now, all that remains are the circus wagons at the
edge of town and a darkness that a young man Max
can't seem to shake. As Max investigates the
enchanted circus claims and the Trenchers
abandoned mansion, the line between villains and
sidekicks blurs, and revealing the circus' secrets may
come at the cost of confronting his own.

...

*Buy now at **AmyLSauder.com/Unfixed***

~Couldn't do it without you~

a.k.a. the Acknowledgements

A story is nothing without readers. This particular story wouldn't be what it is if it weren't for some amazing help.

...

Jennifer Esther Wieland, somehow you got the vision before you even read the book. Your fan art made the story come to life. You helped put weapons in the hands of the suspects. You drew more. Then devised more. I so appreciate you.

Yasmeen Hudson: business manager, photo extraordinaire, partner in [metaphorical and literary] crime. The murderer's first guinea pig. Happy unbirthday.

Monica Coleman, you watched me birth the story as the murderer devoured my sleep. The murderer's other first guinea pig. Thanks for your enthusiasm and your friendship.

Josh Long, you were the accidental catalyst for Interview with a Reader. Before that, you agreed to this treacherous 3,000 week adventure. I'm so glad you did.

Courtney Cluney, my research assistant and regular dose of extroversion. You sacrificed many vampire dates for this story. And helped make a mind-blowing ending. Always & forever.

Megan Fatheree, who pointed out all the places that need fanfiction. (Psst, someone please write it now, k thanks.)

Olivia J. Bennett, totally tracking with the story until my underwhelming draft ending. I'm so sorry. So sorry. I ripped your heart out, and not in the good authorly way. Your feedback made the ending better. Thanks for sticking with me.

Stephanie Gagnon, the first reader to wholeheartedly buy into the ending. You made me believe in an audience for this book.

Amber Lisa Marie Davis, for being the first reader to guess the ending. I like the way your mind works, ya know.

Becca Reedy, was it counting commas or apostrophes? I can't remember. Either way, your dedication is astounding. I couldn't ask for a more committed beta reader.

Hope and Abigail Keane, fangirls before I had any writing to show for it. Thanks for suggesting poisonous material believably in a theater. Woohoo for gruesome death planning!

Mom and Dad, believing in my writing when I thought I knew something about writing but was still learning. I'm still learning, but I think it might be worth reading now maybe?

Ksenia Anske, you made my dream tangible. I've looked to you for what my writerly career would/could look like. Your creative philosophy, stories, and guidance are incomparable.

L. L. Bayird, for all your time trying to fix your computer to send feedback. Thank you for all your efforts and support.

Jessica Doble, for understanding my inspiration, Italo Calvino.

Italo Calvino. The spark was there before, but you turned my love of second person storytelling into a blazing inferno.

...

Undying gratitude to those who endured jarring transitions, glaring typos, atrocious rabbit trails, plotholes, and more. Each of you brought changes to the story, some even with pages of thorough thoughts and with multiple readings. Thank you for seeing the story through the weeds and for yanking them out: Kim Kouski, Paul Maitland, Julia A. Andrews, Jaclyn Lewis, Kathryn Nielson, Heidi Parker, Sarah Dunn, Heather Reid, Tim Reeder, Andy Zach, Timothy Schellenberg, David Lehnert, Linda Heller, Jennifer Rehn, Sarah Foster, Kayla Parshall, Éowyn Lewis, Dyana Hulgan, Noreen Karcher, and Jodie DuCharme.

...

And to you, reader. You leave your mark on each book you touch. Making it your own. Adding to the story what is absent from the page. You're pure magic.

~We did it!~

~Liked it? Or didn't?~

The book world needs you!

...

Lend the superpowers of an honest review on Goodreads, Amazon, your social media, wherever. Your reviews help readers choose a book they'll enjoy, and help authors find their readers. It's a win-win-win-win-win-win... You get the picture.

...

~Be the reviewer~
~the world needs today~

~The party ain't over~

Tag your fanfiction, fanart, & headcanon:

#IKYLAM

Send it my way:
Website: AmyLSauder.com
Facebook: /AmyLSauder
Instagram: @AmyLSauderCreations
Twitter: @AmyLSauder
Email: AmyLSauder@gmail.com

~Read This First~

Dearest reader, take heed!

...

It is one of my fondest predispositions to read the last sentence of a book first. It hints at closure, yet nearly never gives away something of import.

...

However, should you be of similar disposition, you may greatly regret doing so with this story.

...

~This tale ends with a bang~

www.ingramcontent.com/pod-product-compliance
Lightning Source LLC
Chambersburg PA
CBHW071134100726
47908CB00008B/2598